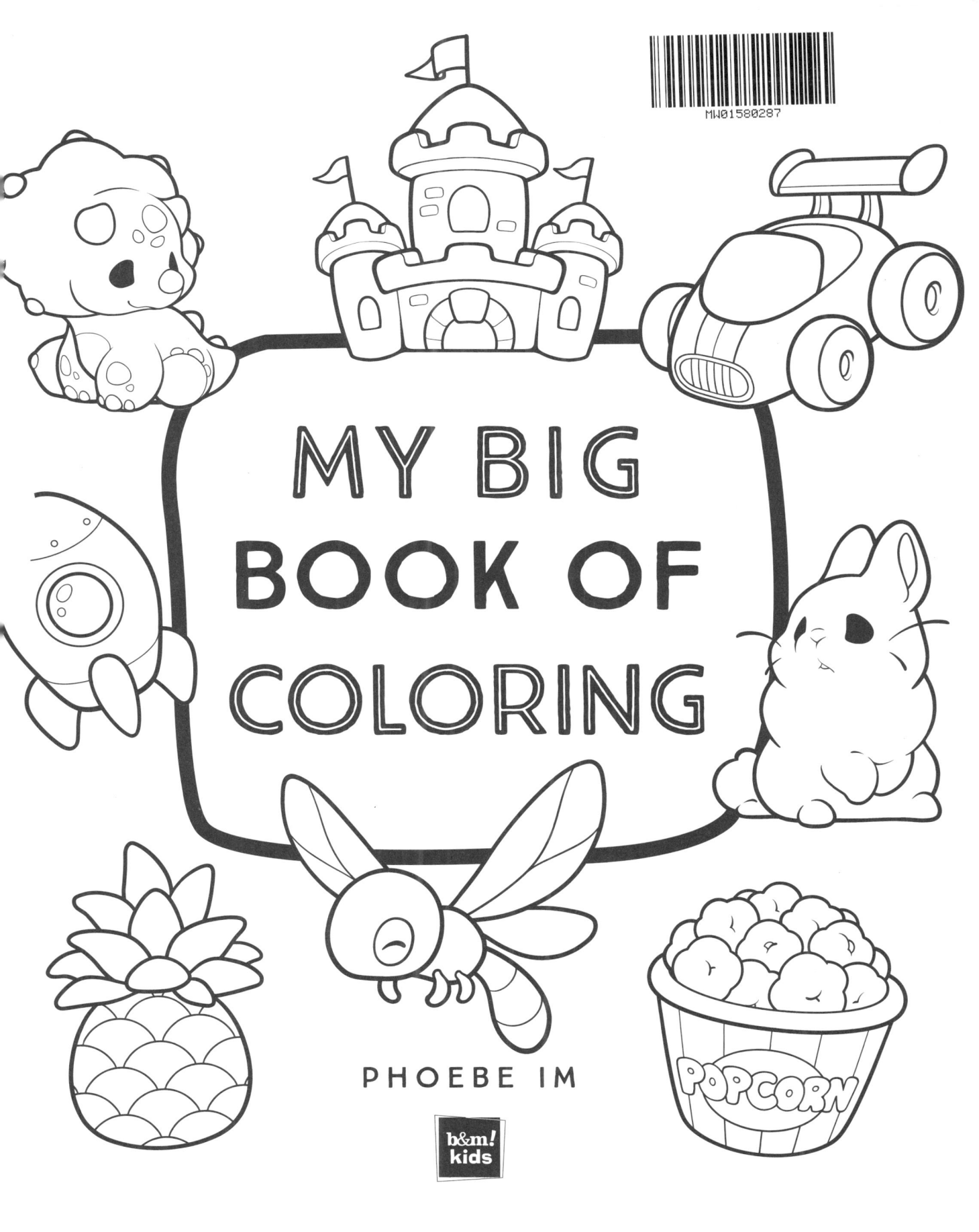

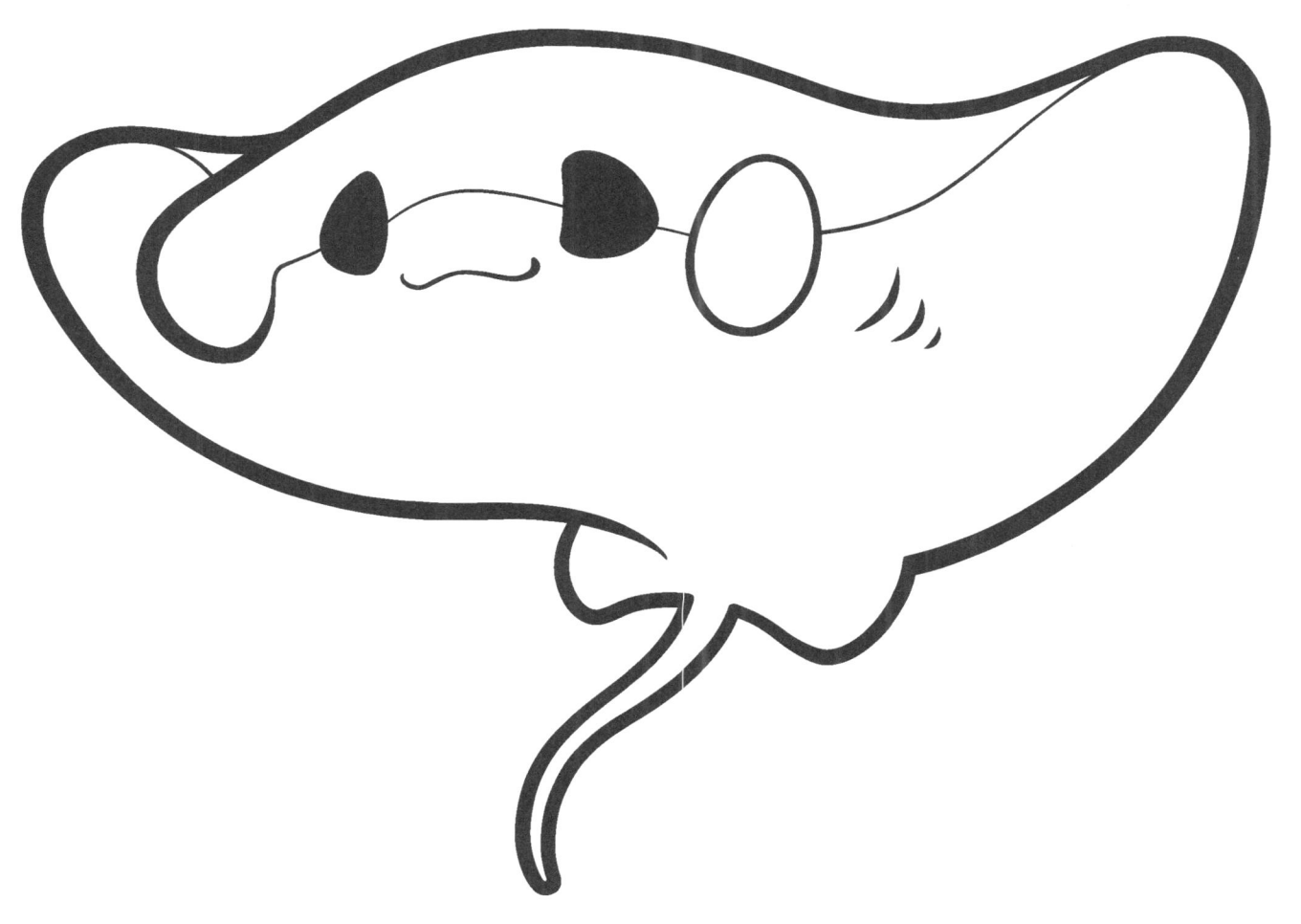

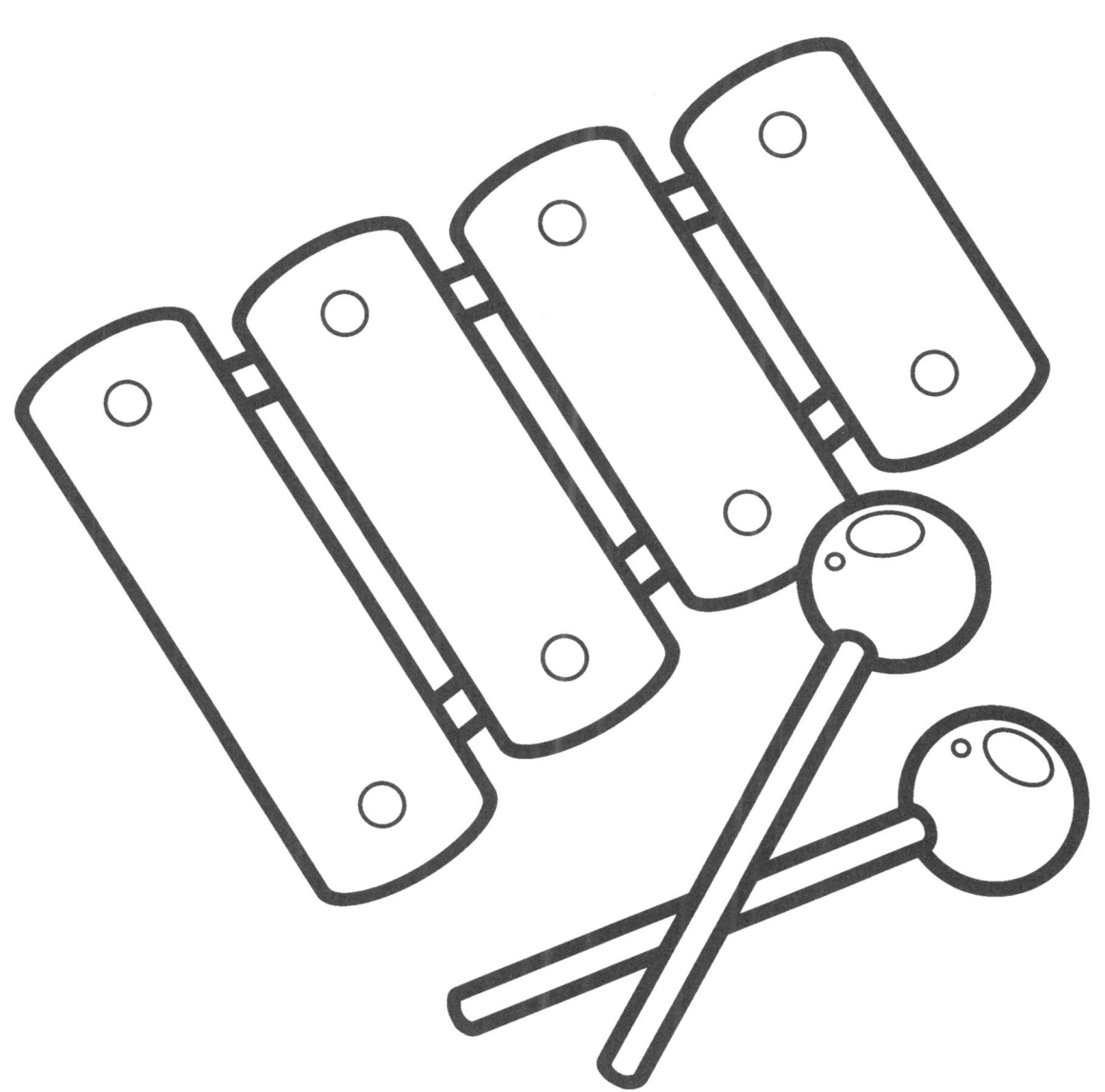

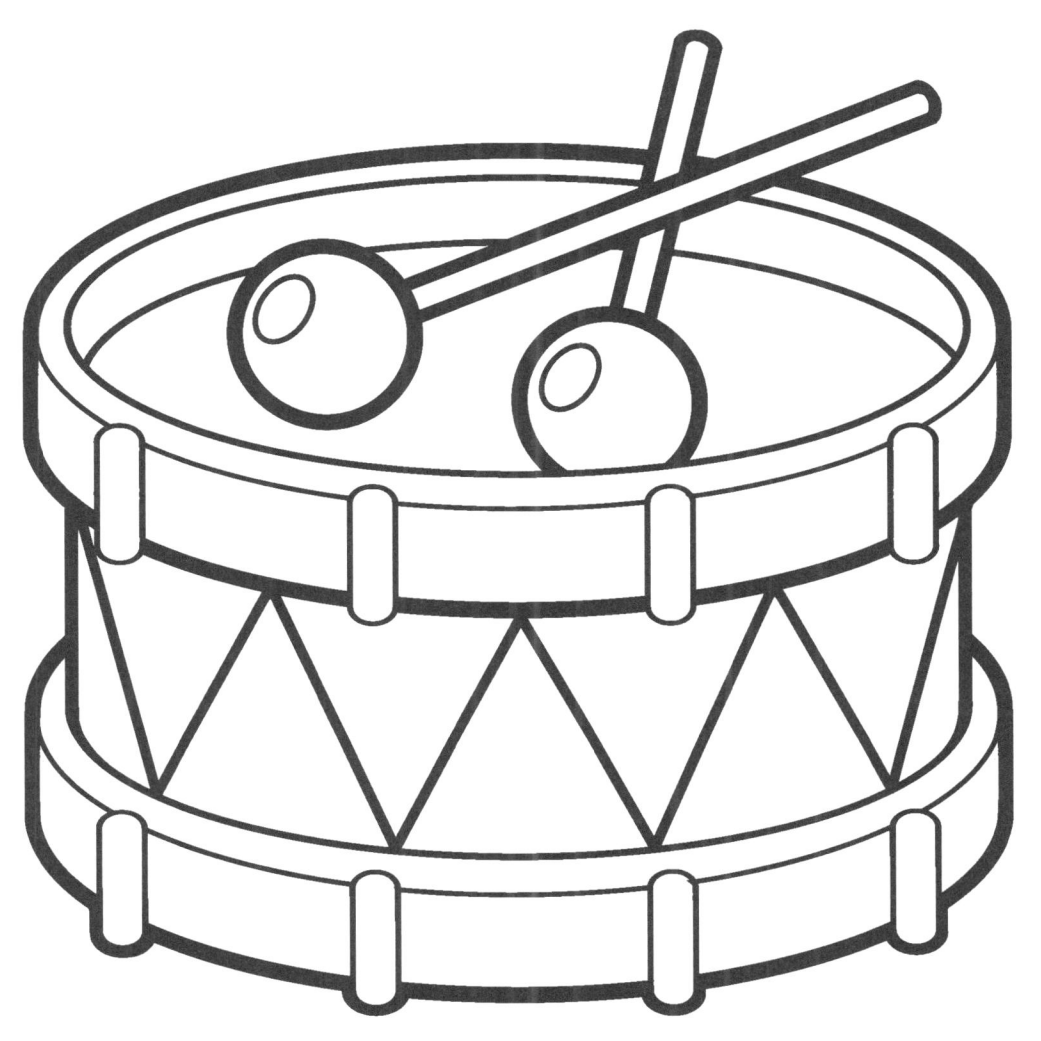

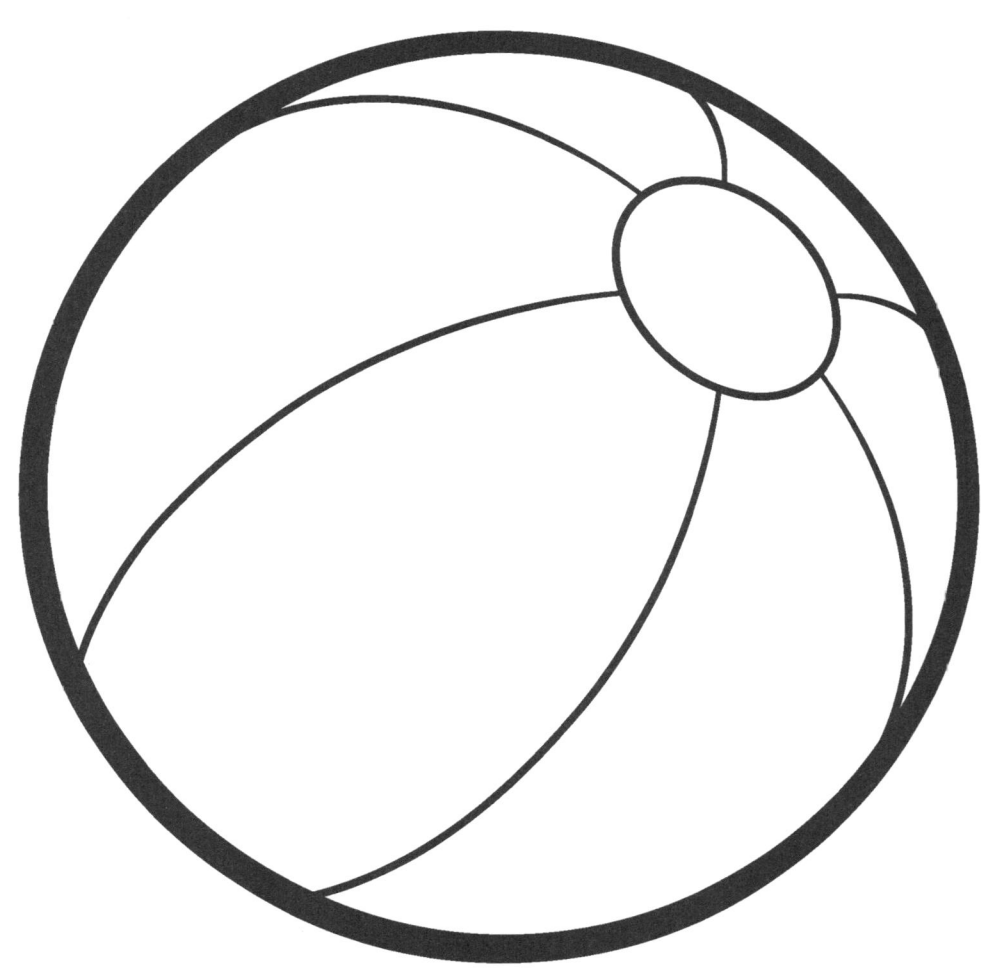

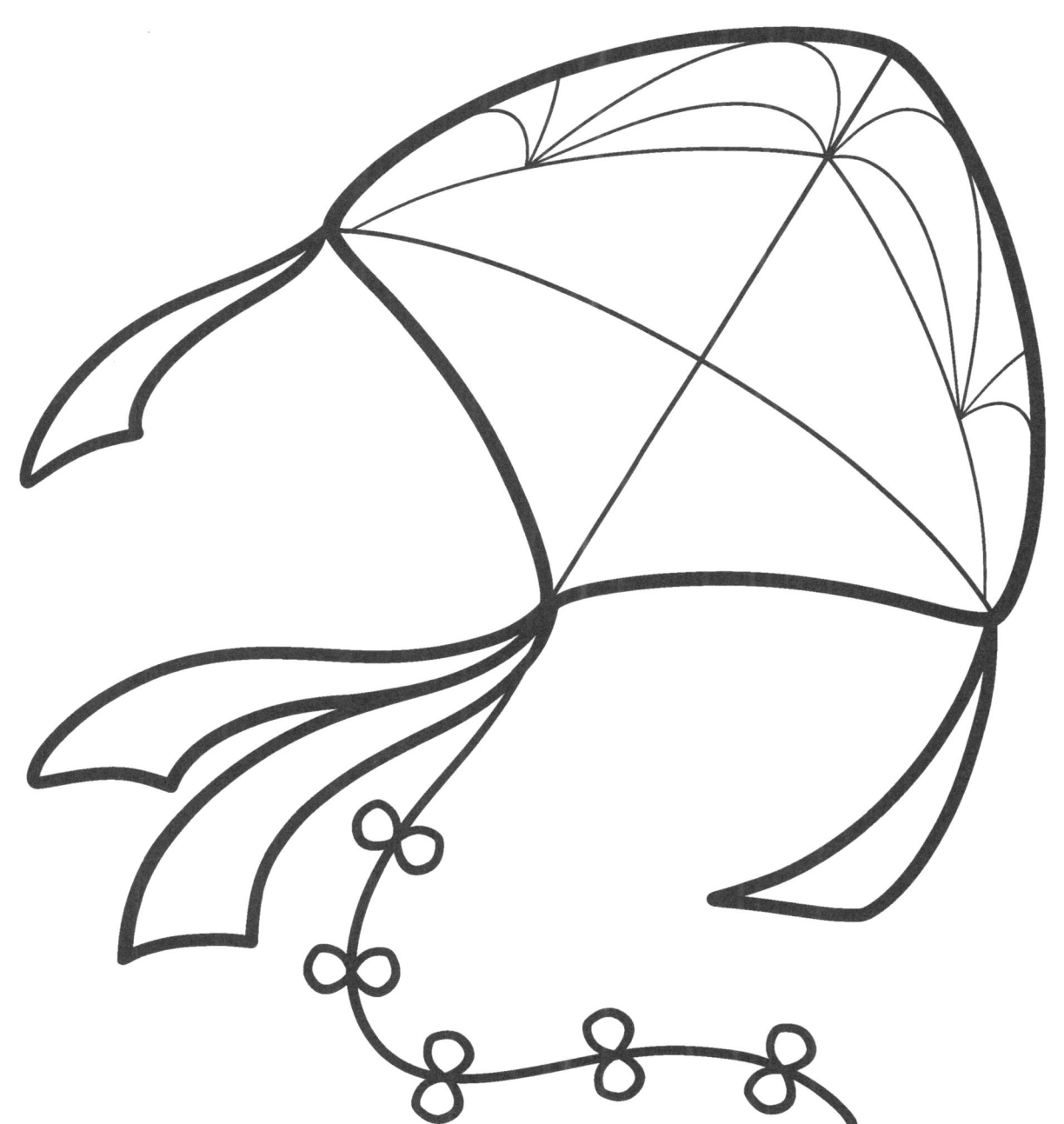

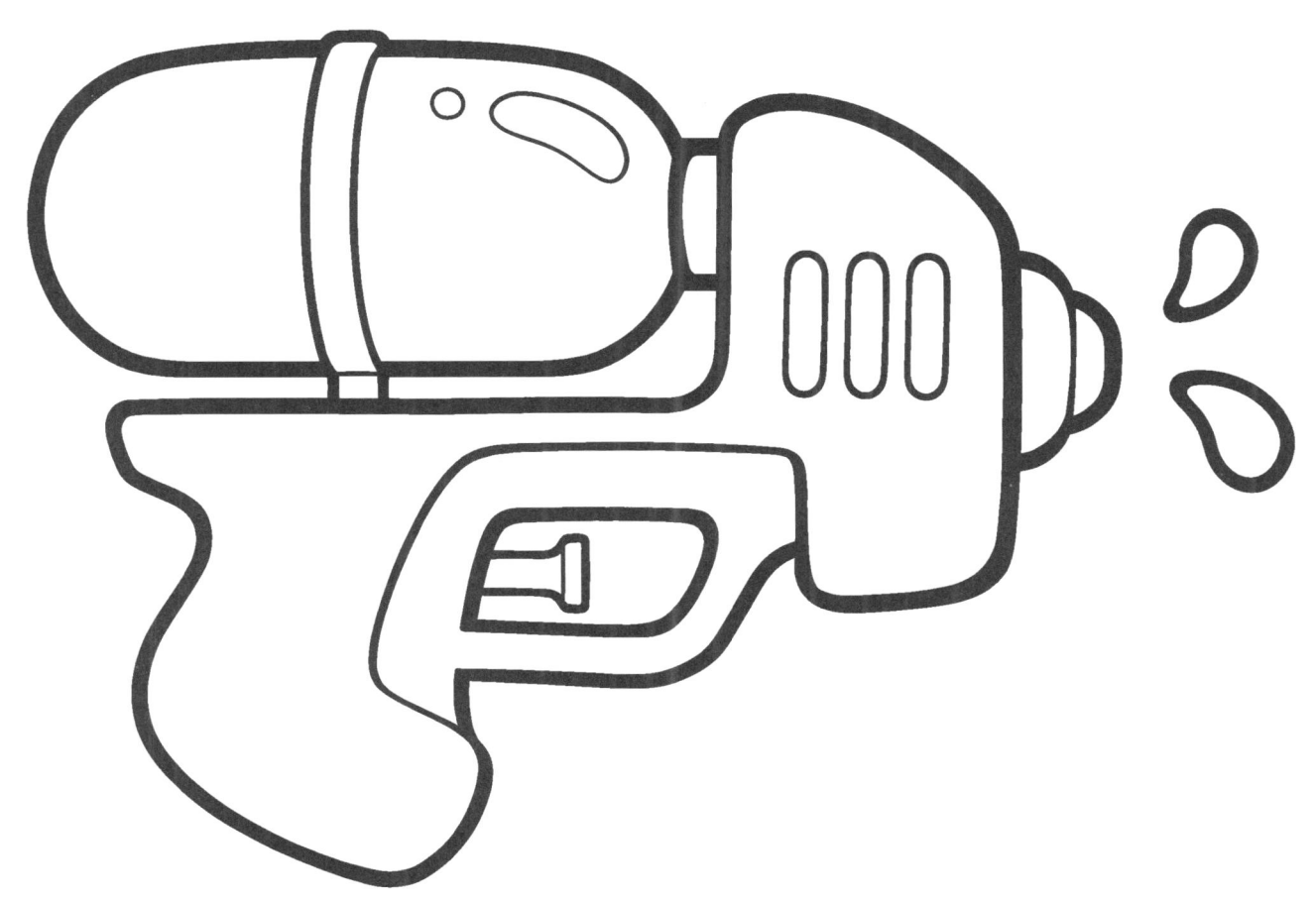

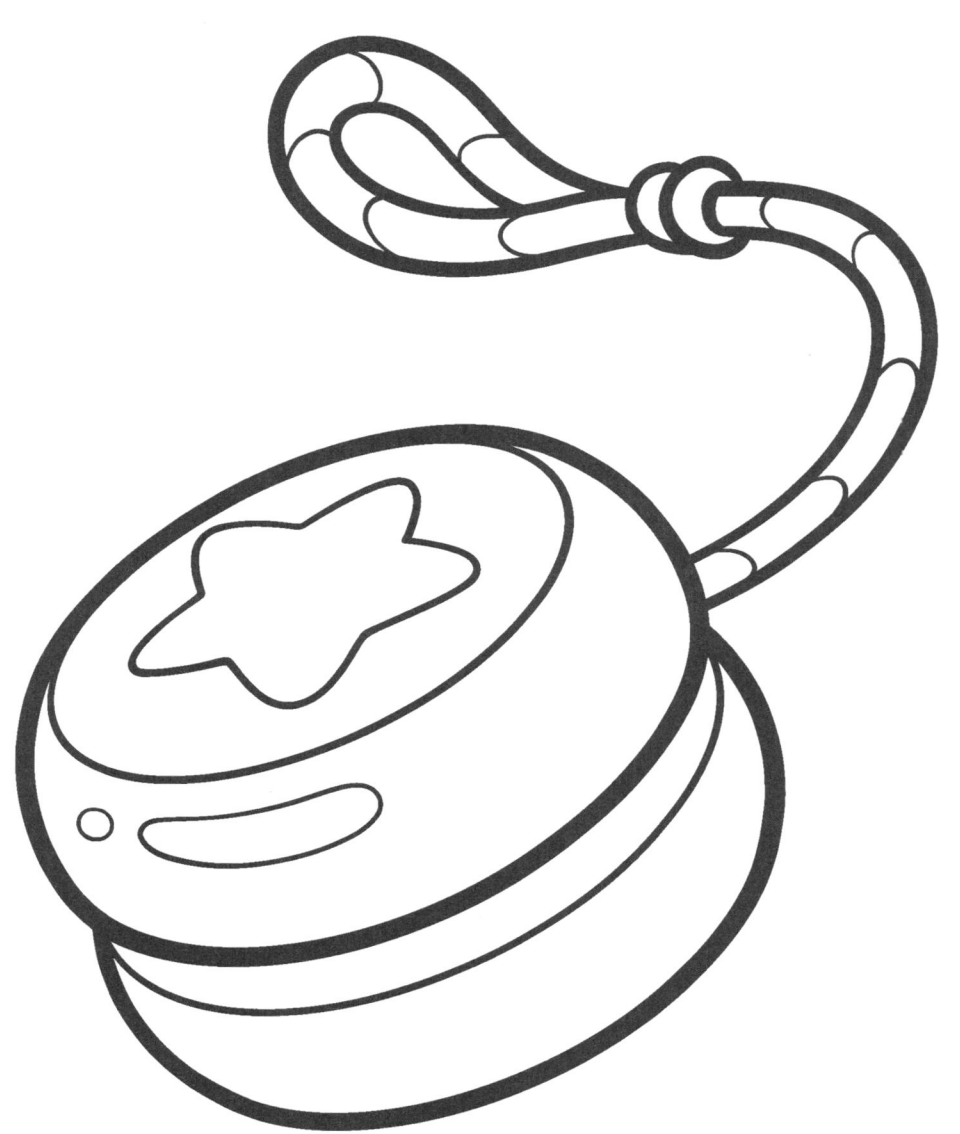

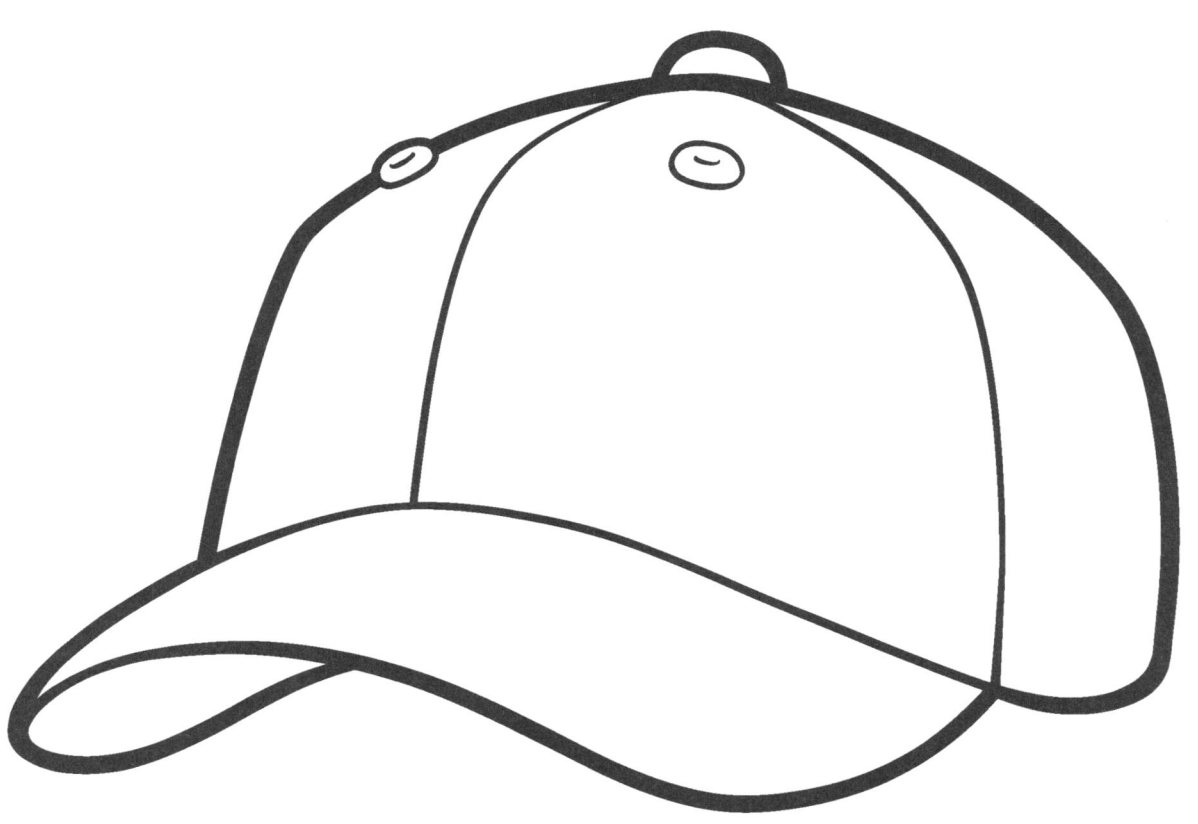

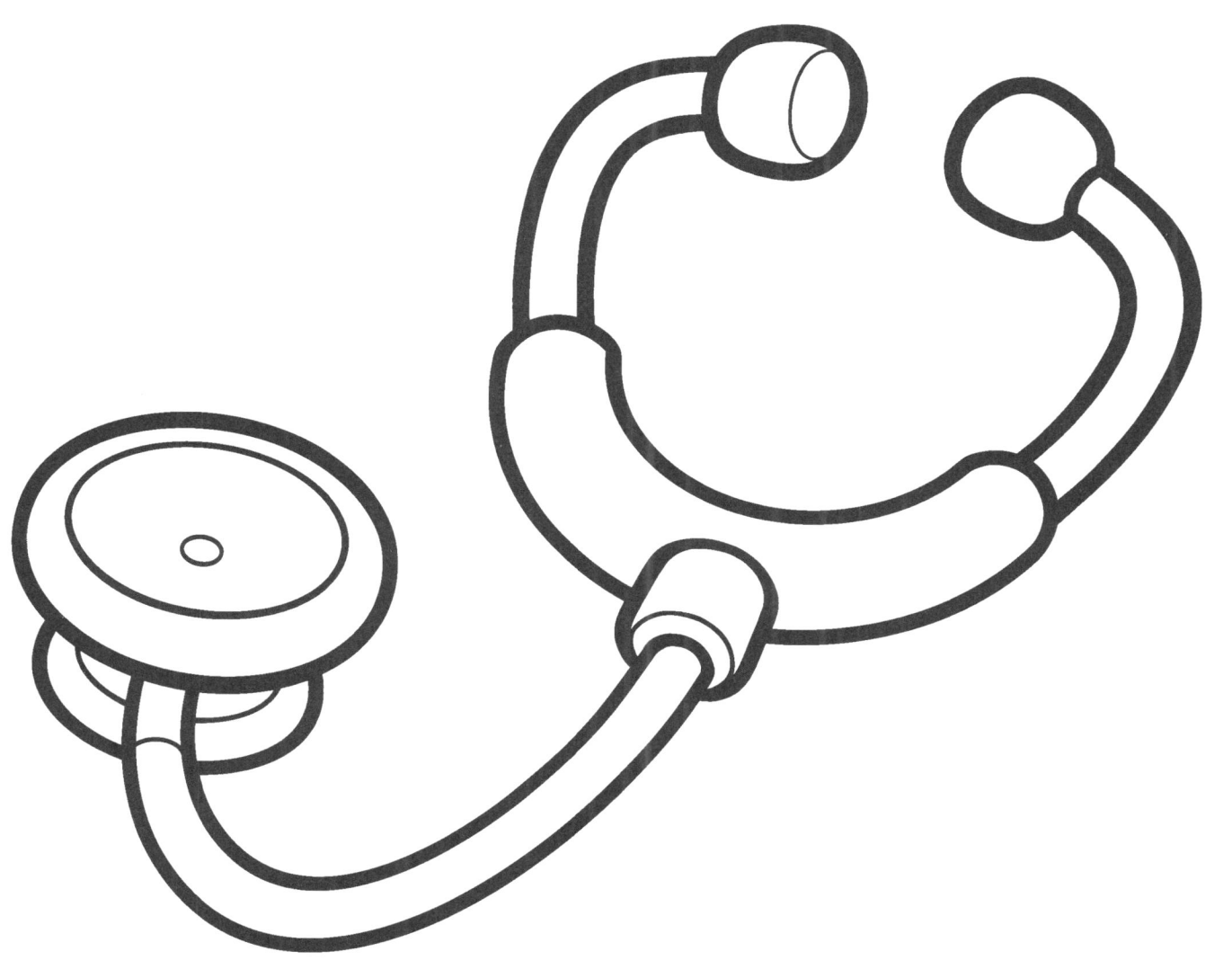

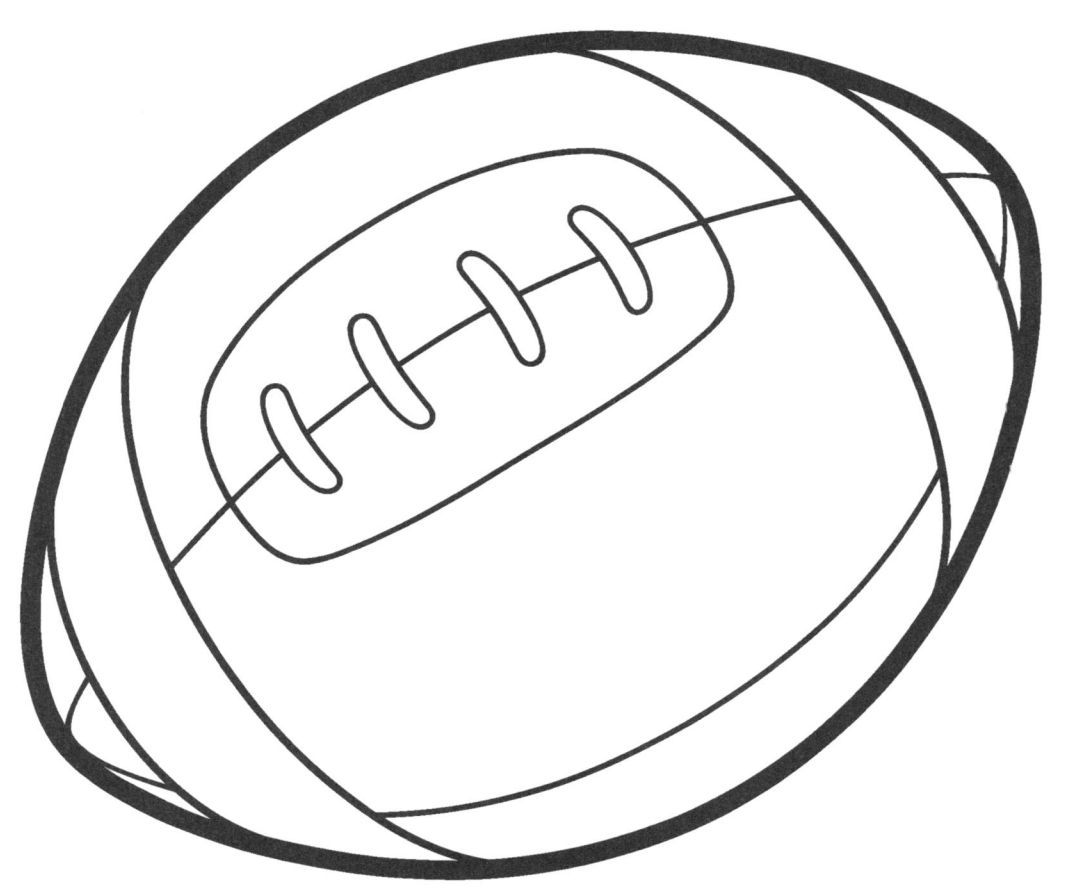

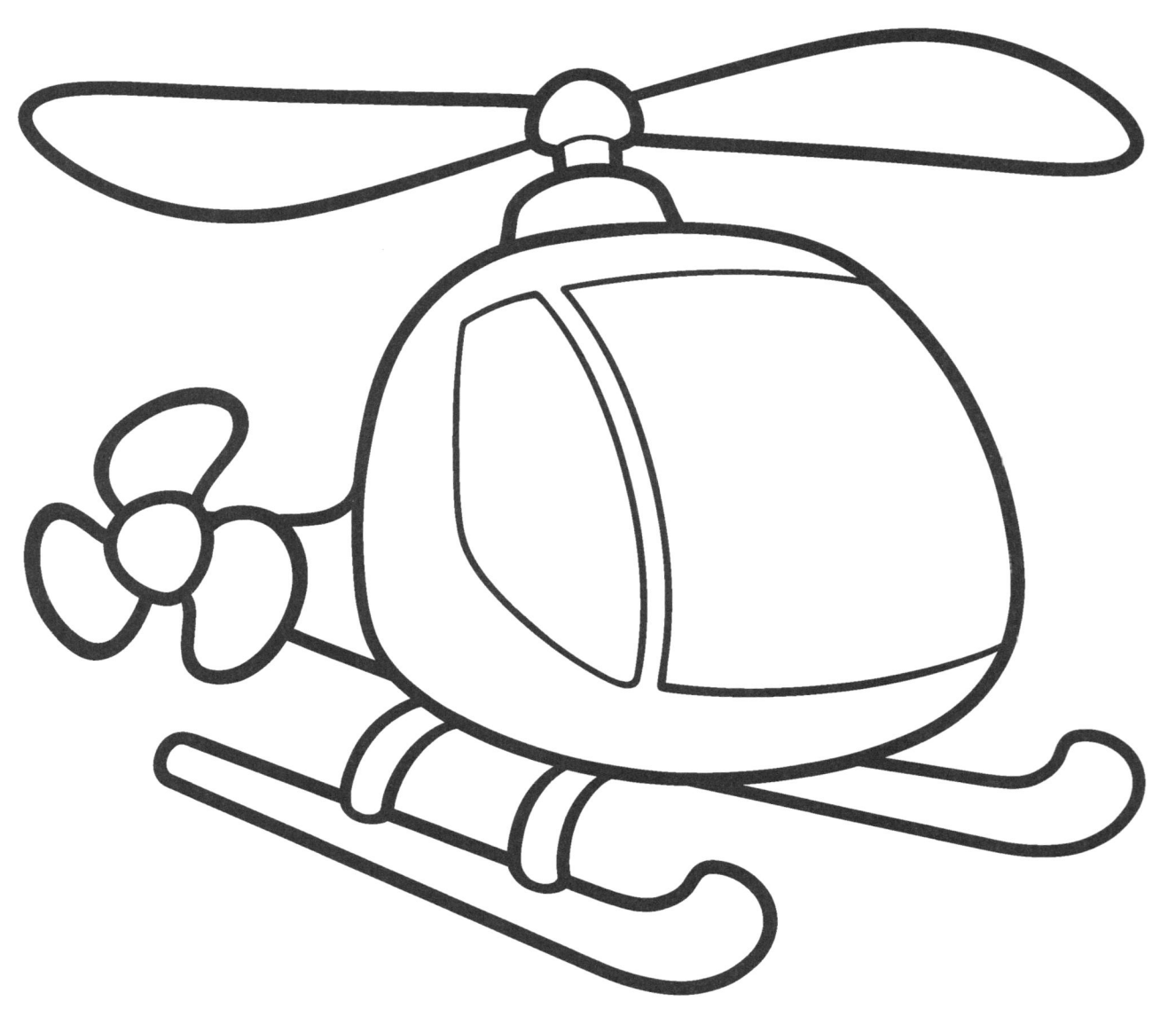

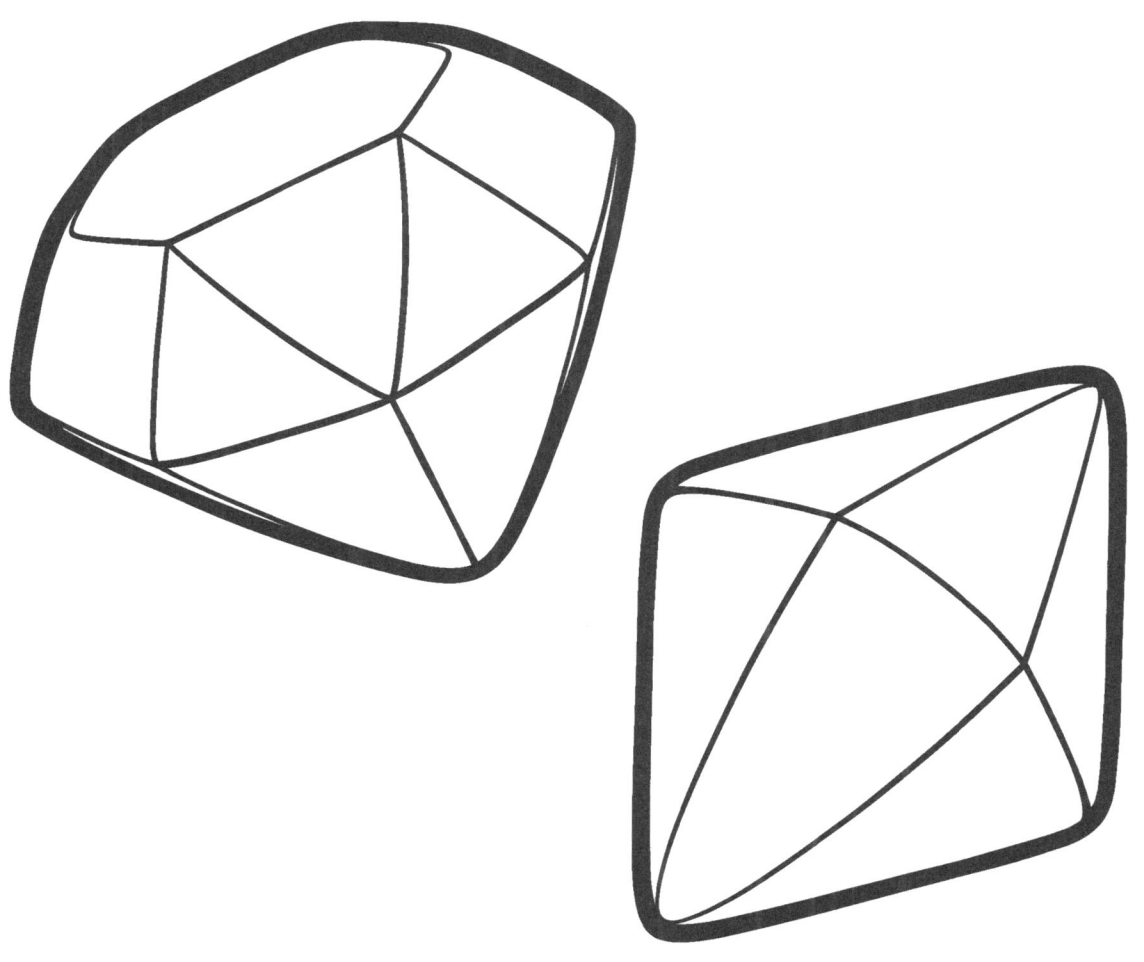

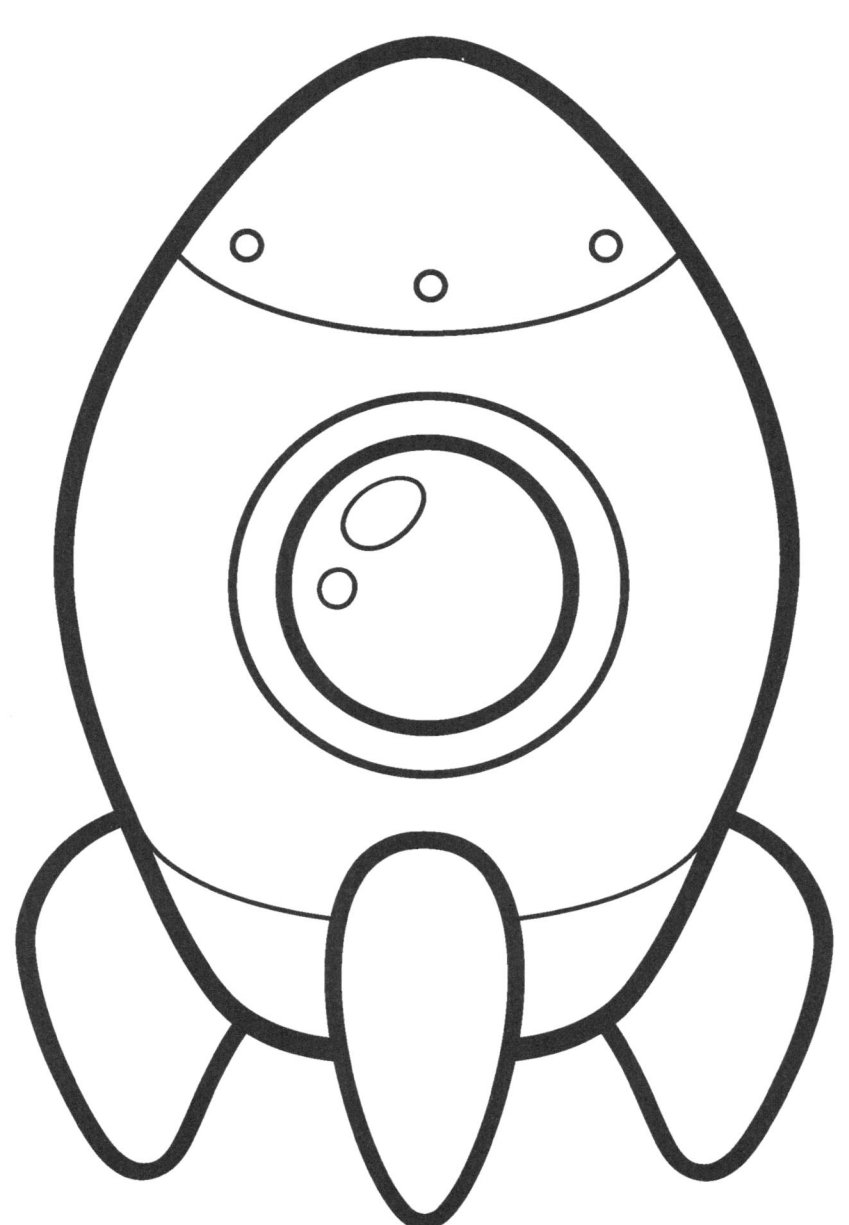

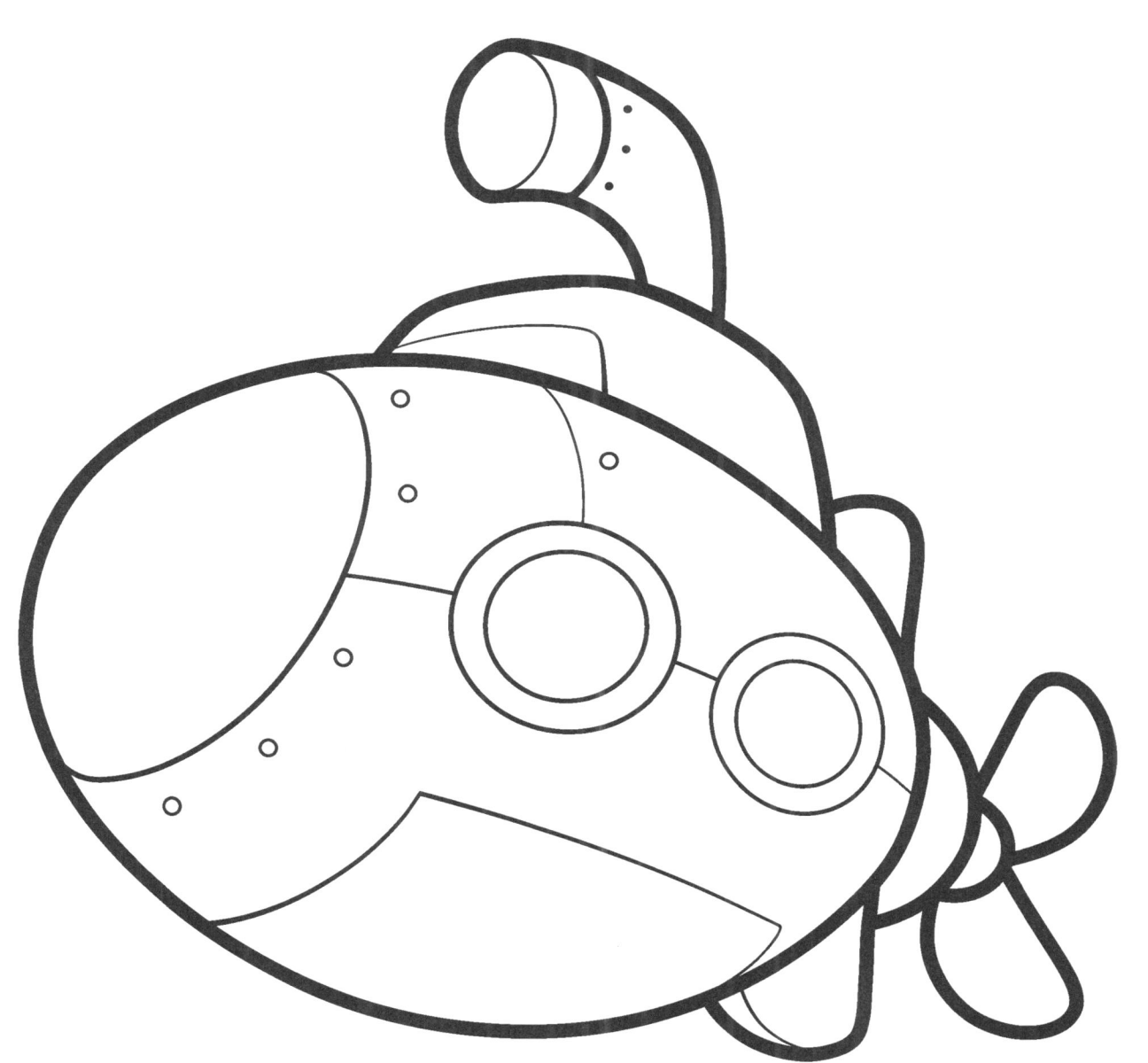

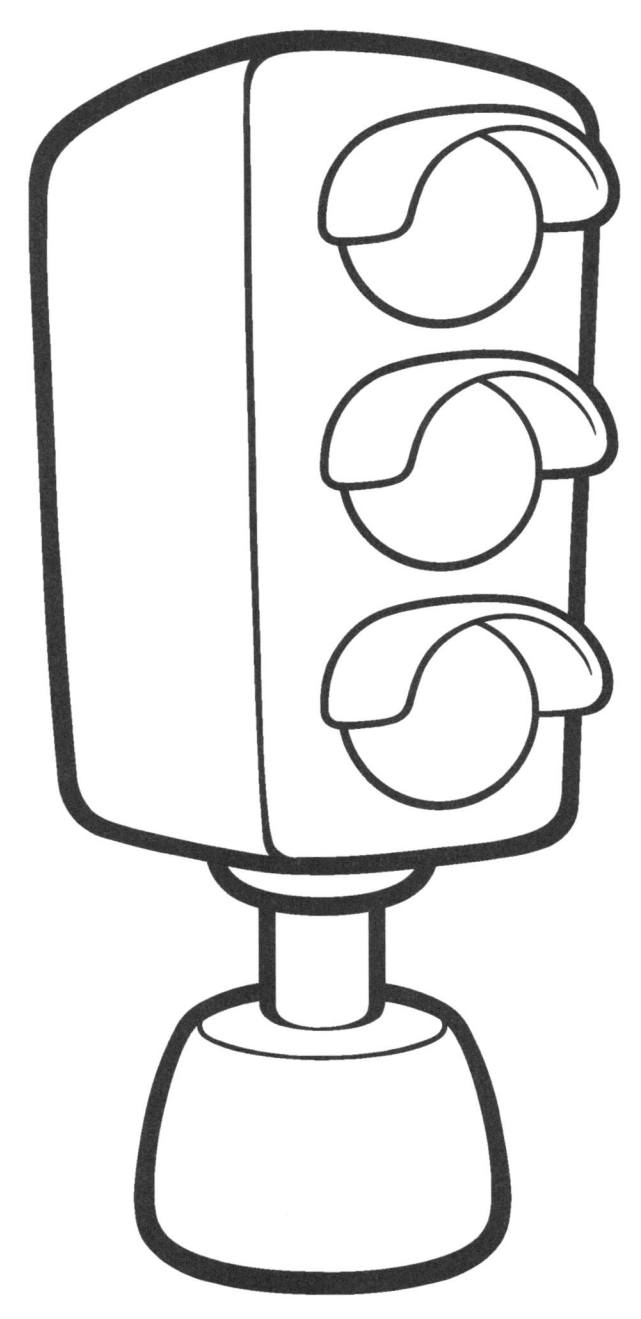

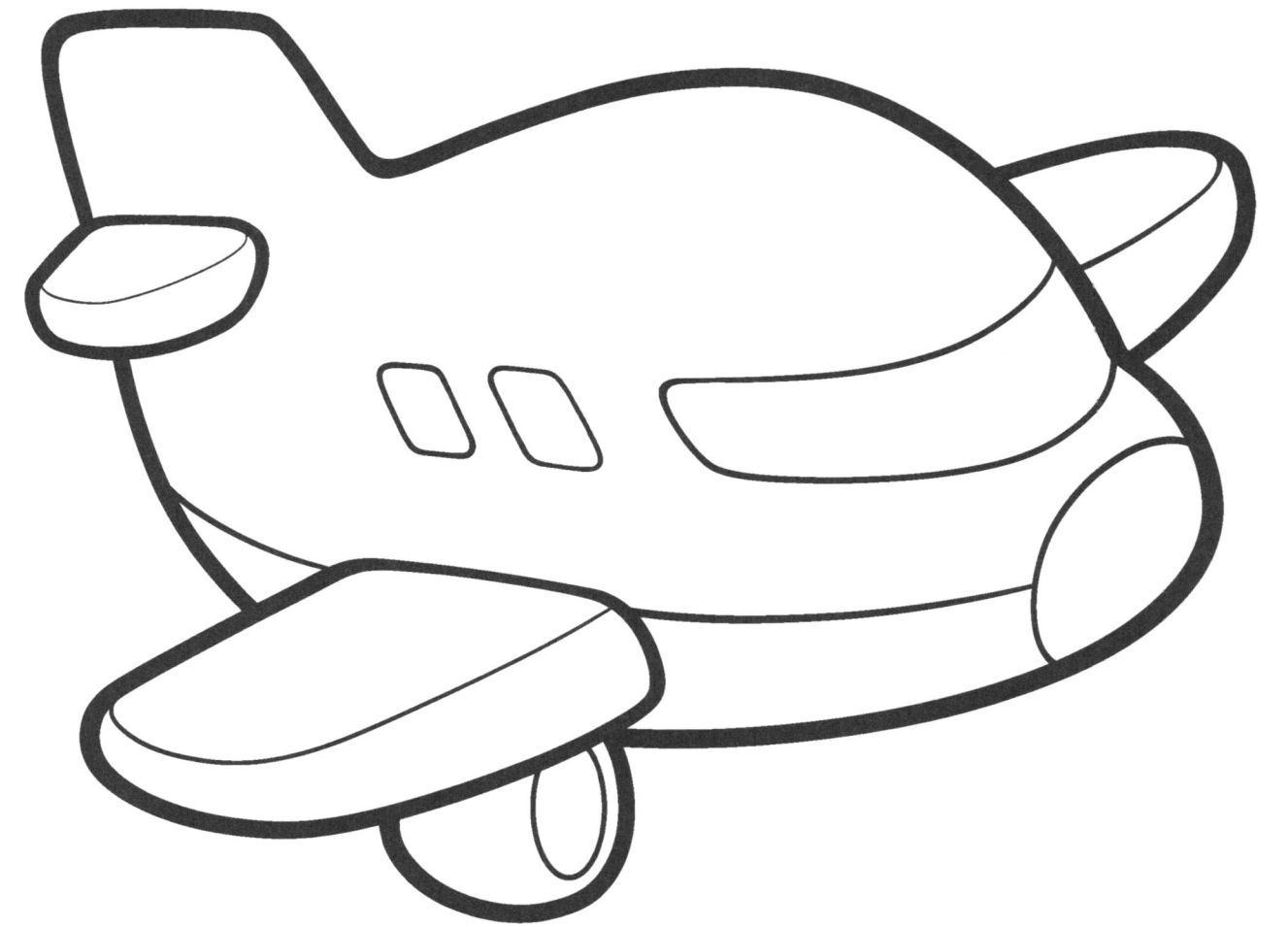

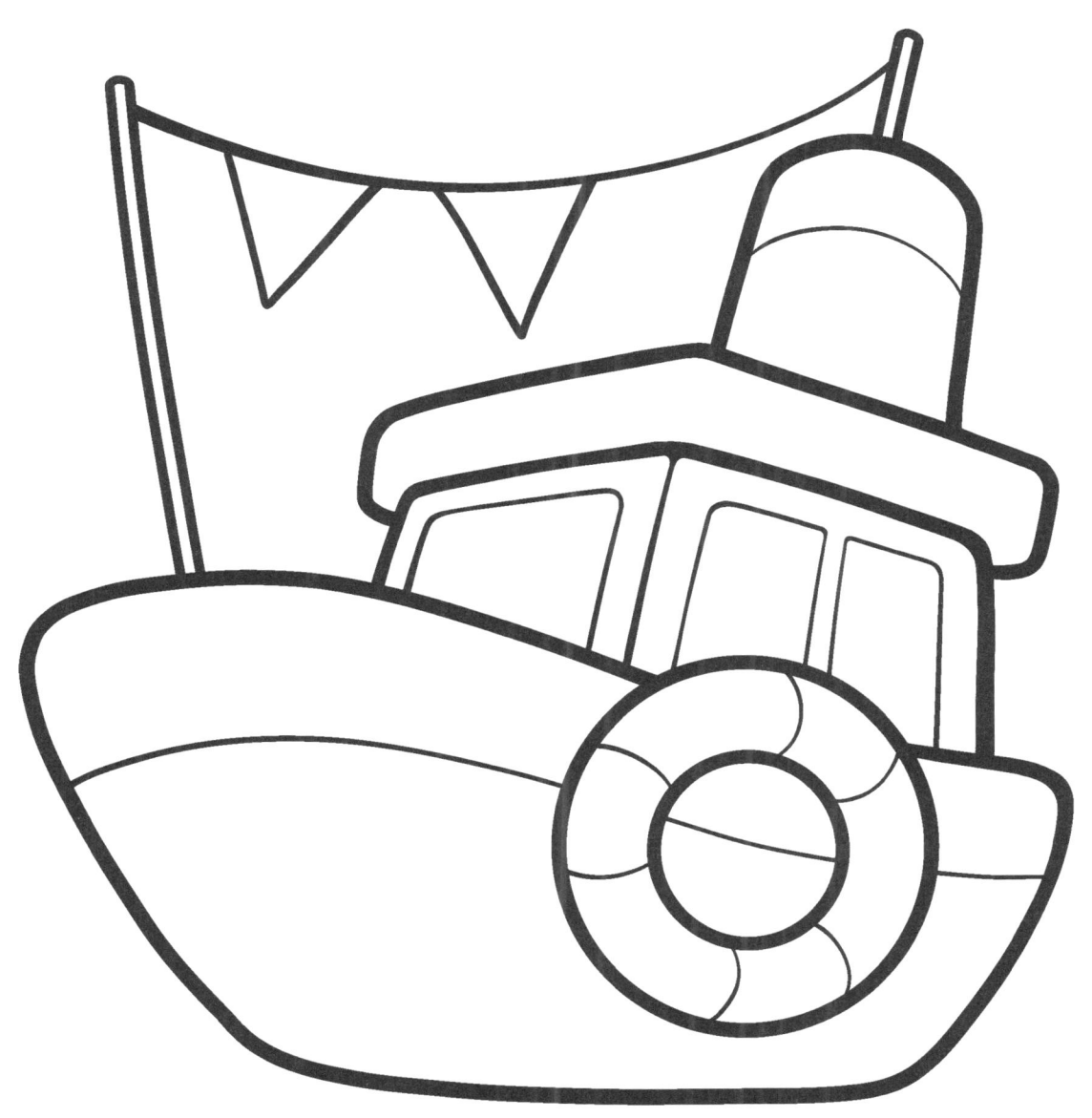

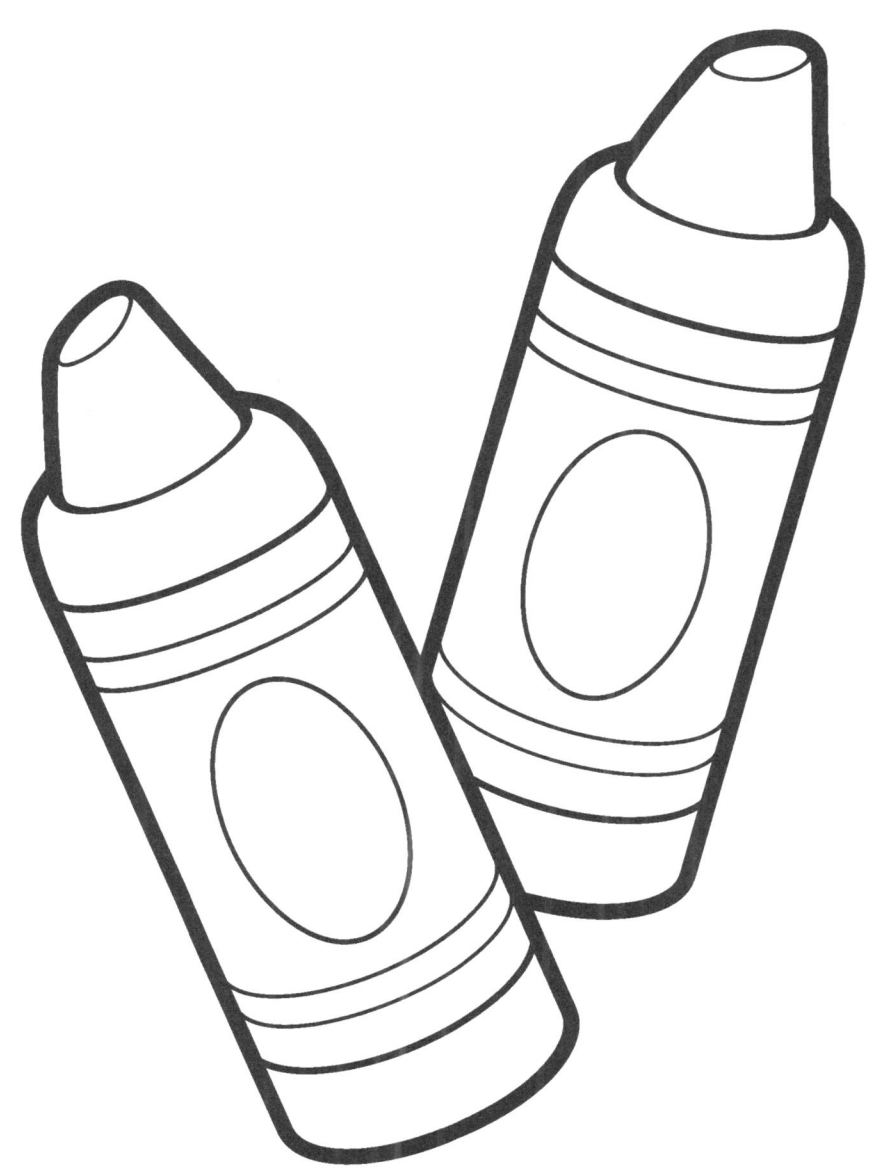

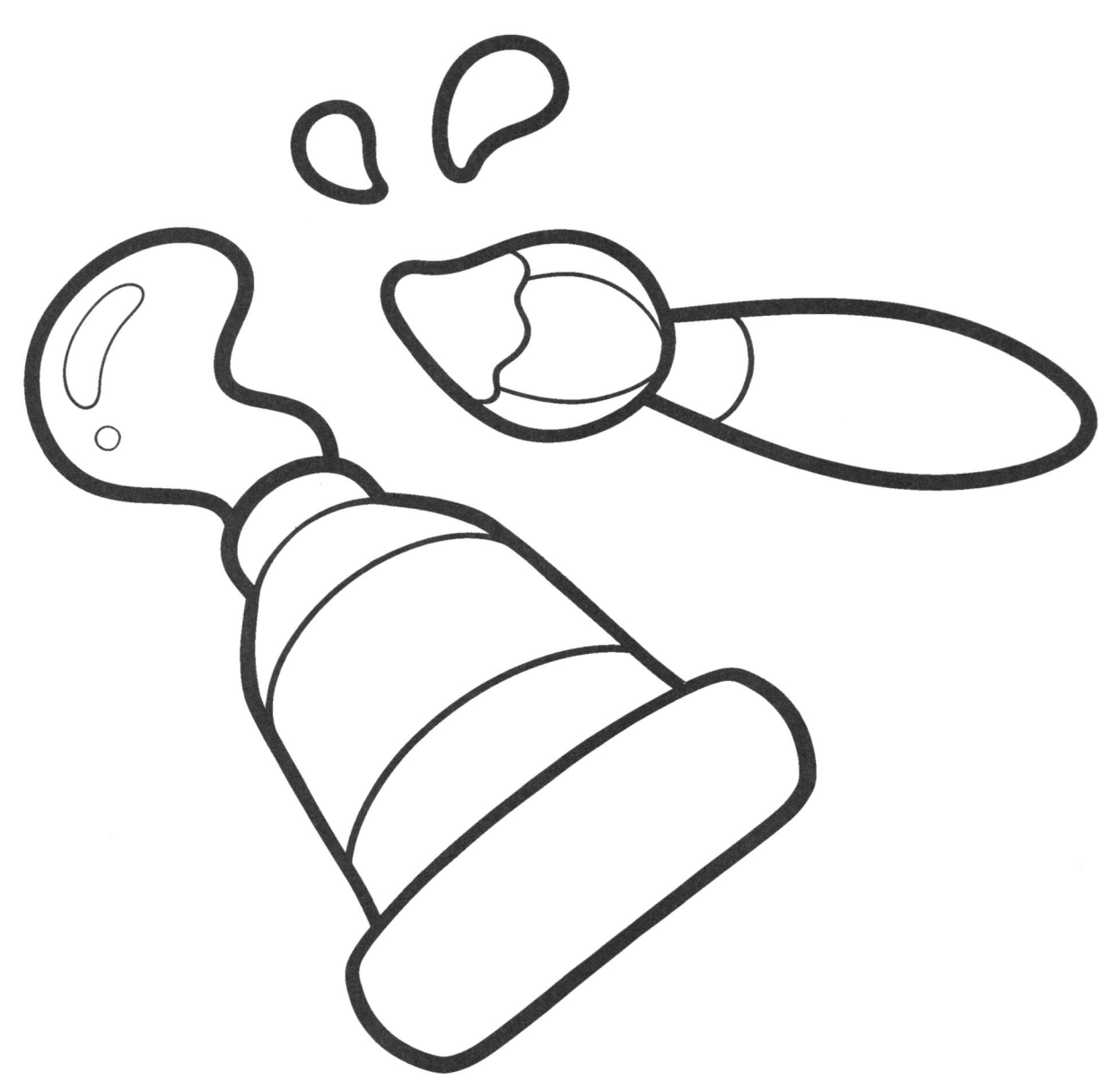

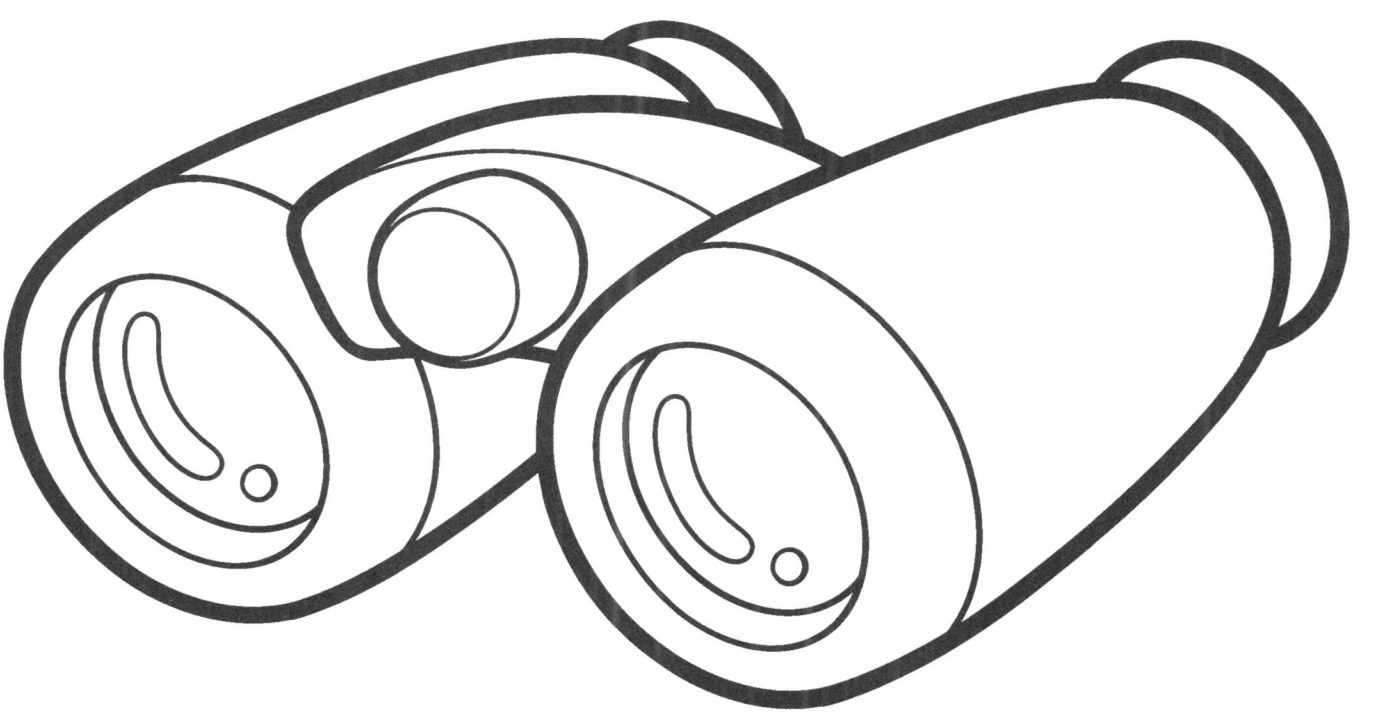

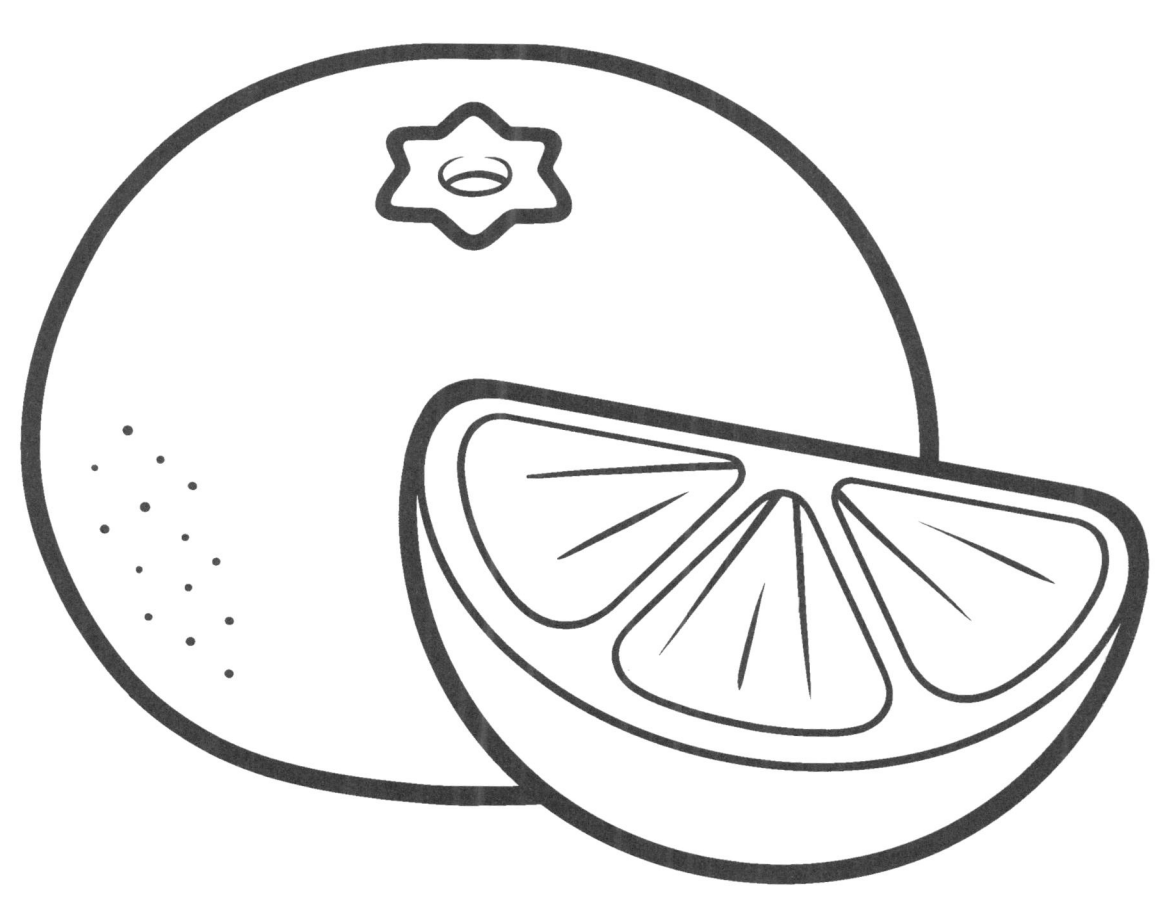

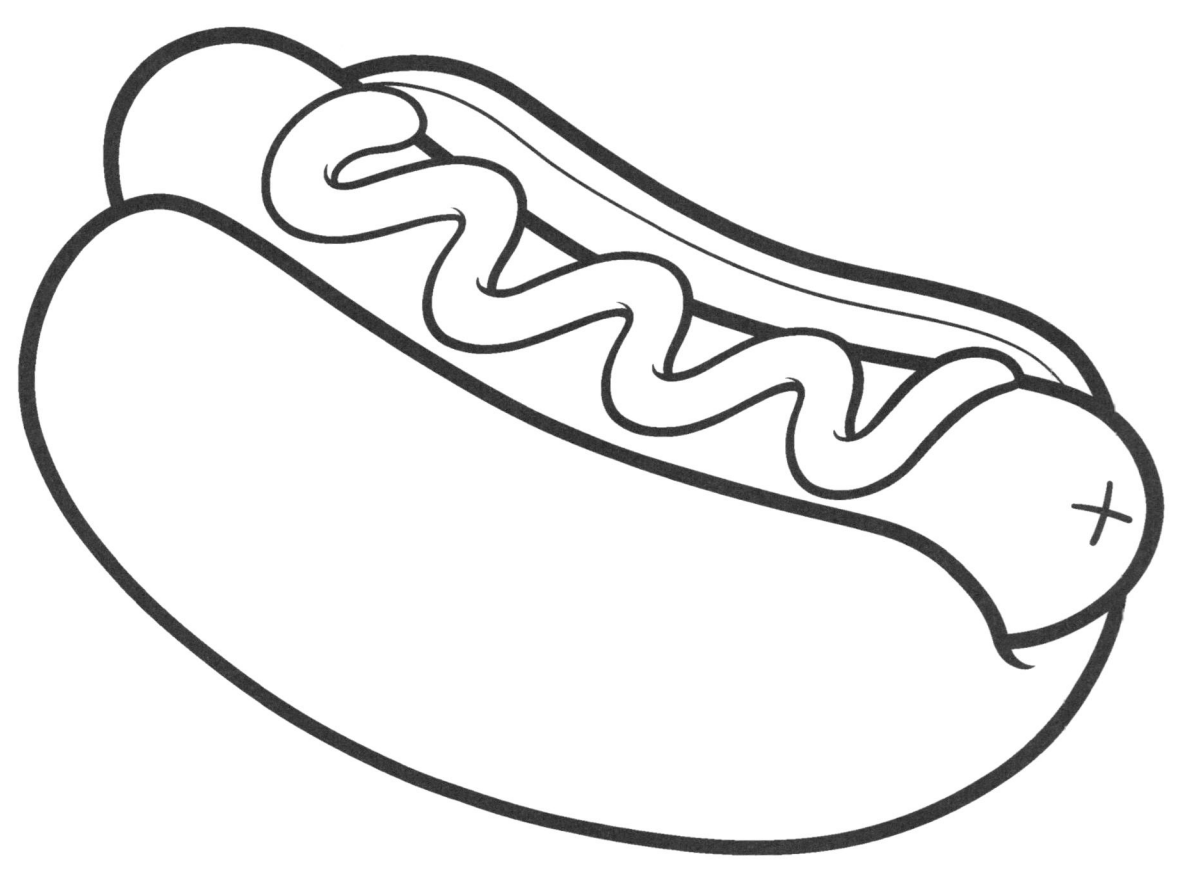

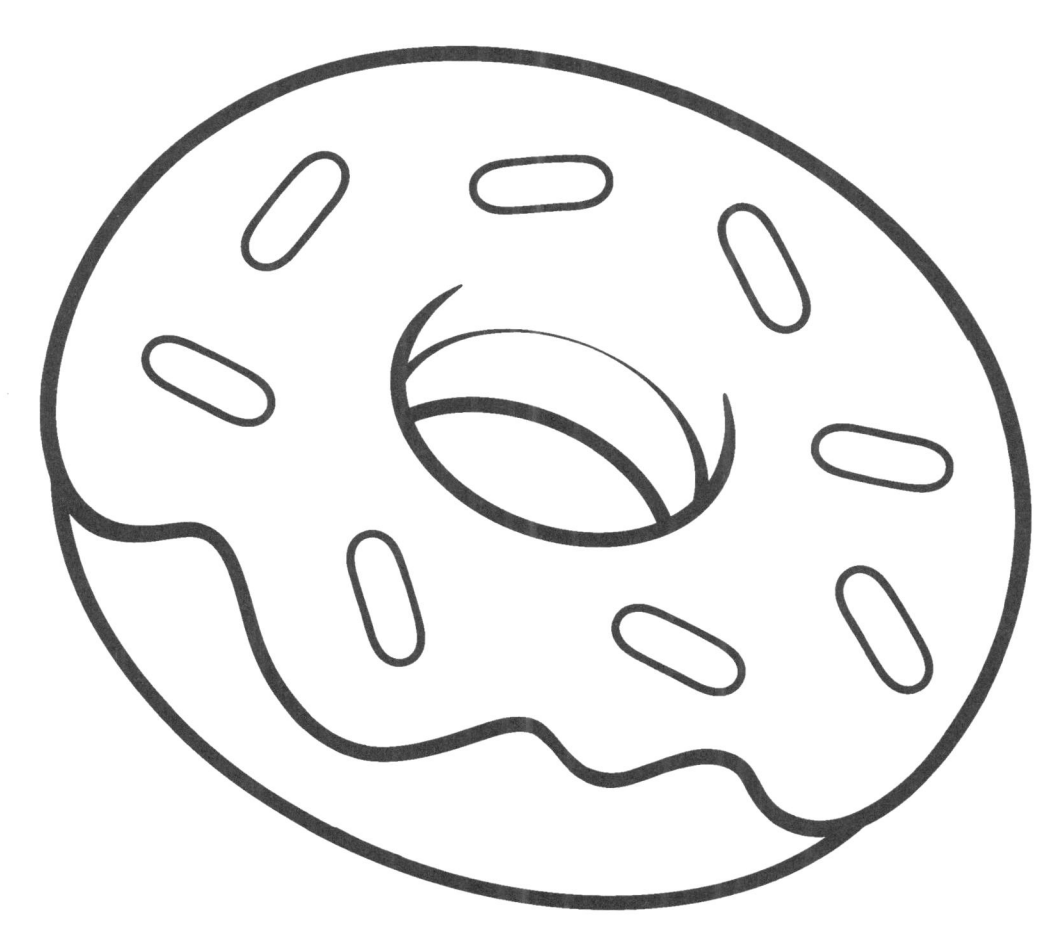

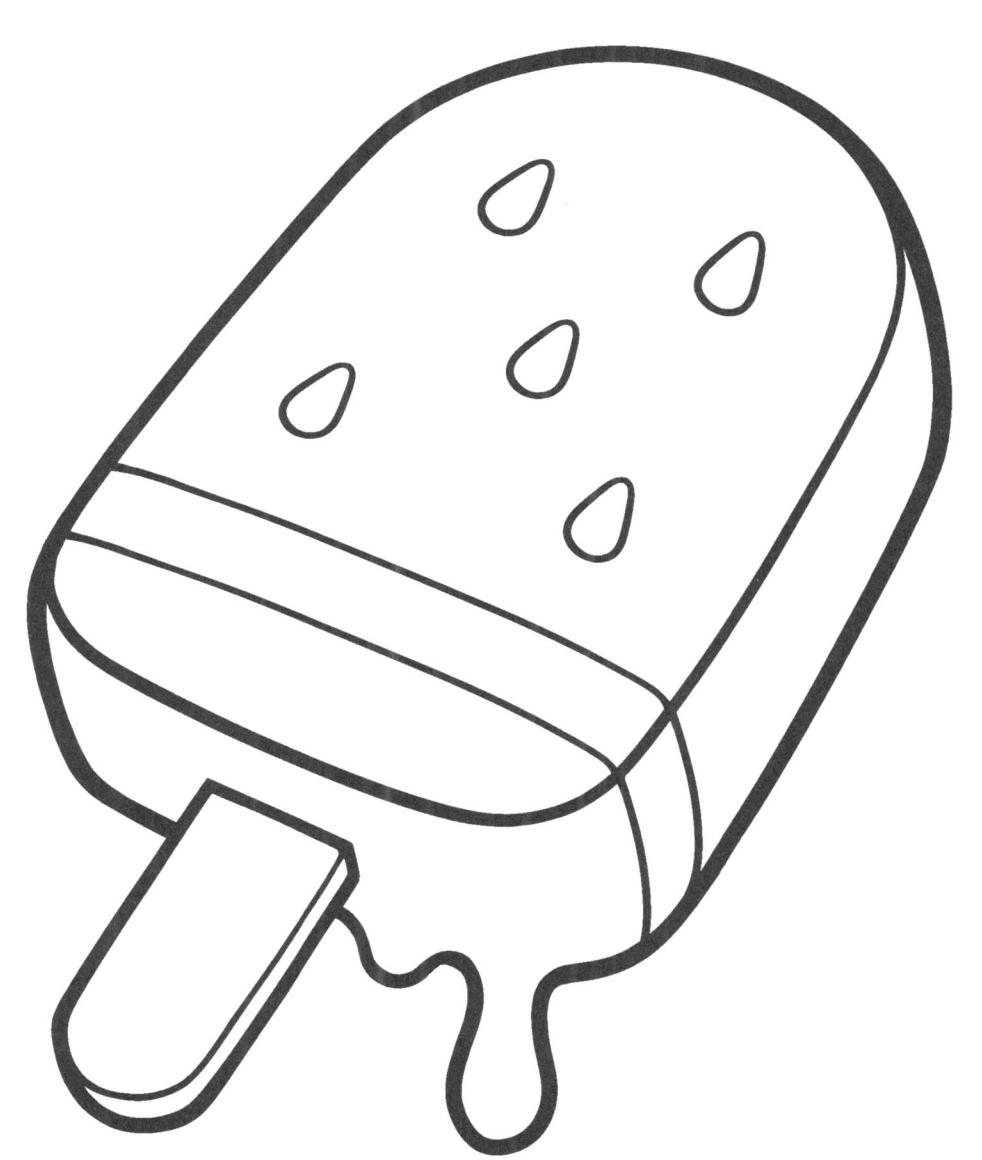

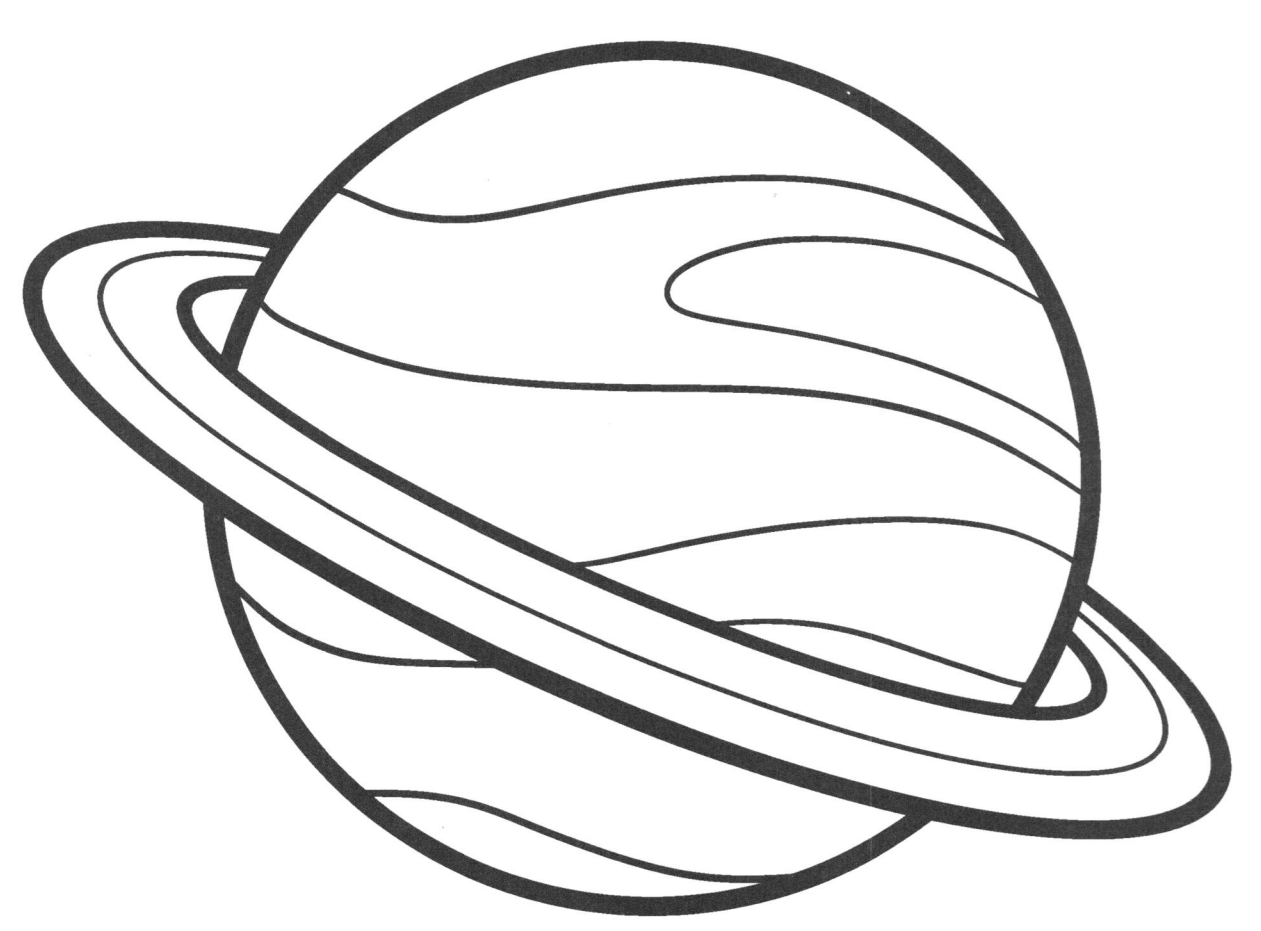

© 2025 by Quarto Publishing Group USA Inc.

First published in 2025 by becker&mayer!kids, an imprint of The Quarto Group,
142 West 36th Street, 4th Floor, New York, NY 10018, USA
(212) 779-4972 www.Quarto.com

All rights reserved. No part of this book may be reproduced in any form without written permission of the copyright owners. All images included in this book are original works created by the artist credited on the copyright page, not generated by artificial intelligence, and have been reproduced with the knowledge and prior consent of the artist. The producer, publisher, and printer accept no responsibility for any infringement of copyright or otherwise arising from the contents of this publication. Every effort has been made to ensure that credits accurately comply with the information supplied. We apologize for any inaccuracies that may have occurred and will address inaccurate or missing information in a subsequent reprinting of the book

becker&mayer!kids titles are also available at discount for retail, wholesale, promotional, and bulk purchase.
For details, contact the Special Sales Manager by email at specialsales@quarto.com or by mail at
The Quarto Group, Attn: Special Sales Manager, 100 Cummings Center Suite 265D, Beverly, MA 01915 USA.

10 9 8 7 6 5 4 3 2 1

ISBN: 978-0-7603-9931-6

Group Publisher: Rage Kindelsperger
Creative Director: Laura Drew
Managing Editor: Cara Donaldson
Cover Design: Laura Drew
Illustrations: Phoebe Im

Printed in China